For Sam Ryan,
beautiful inside
and out J.W.

First published in Great Britain in 2016 by Andersen Press Ltd.,
20 Vauxhall Bridge Road, London SWIV 2SA.
Text copyright © Jeanne Willis, 2016. Illustration copyright ©Tony Ross 2016.
The rights of Jeanne Willis and Tony Ross to be identified as the author
and illustrator of this work have been asserted by them in
accordance with the Copyright, Designs and Patents Act, 1988.
Colour separated in Switzerland by Photolitho AG, Zürich.
Printed and bound in China.
First edition
British Library Cataloguing in Publication Data available.
ISBN 978 1 78344 202 7

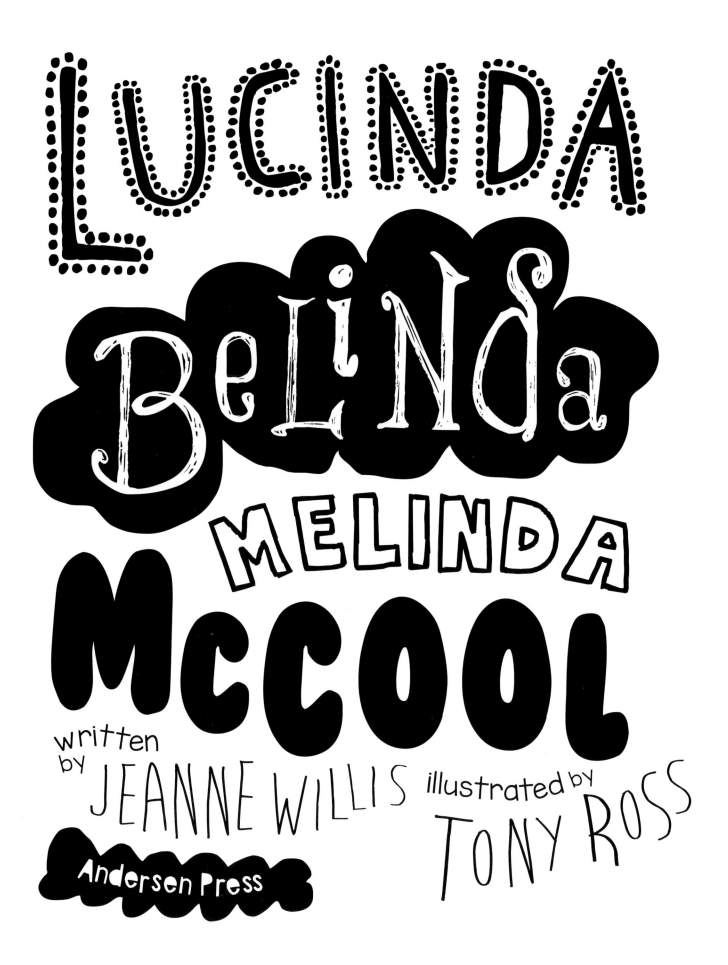

LUCINDA BELINDA MELINDA McCOOL

written by JEANNE WILLIS illustrated by TONY ROSS

Andersen Press

The MOST beautiful
girl in the WHOLE of the
SCHOOL was
LUCINDA BELINDa
MELINDA
McCOOL.

She **dressed** like a **princess** and **smelt** like a rose - she was **perfectly** primped from her **head** to her **toes.**

But Lucinda Belinda felt it was her duty
to guide all her friends in the subject of beauty.
She'd point out their "faults" very loudly in class
and insist they correct them in front of the glass.

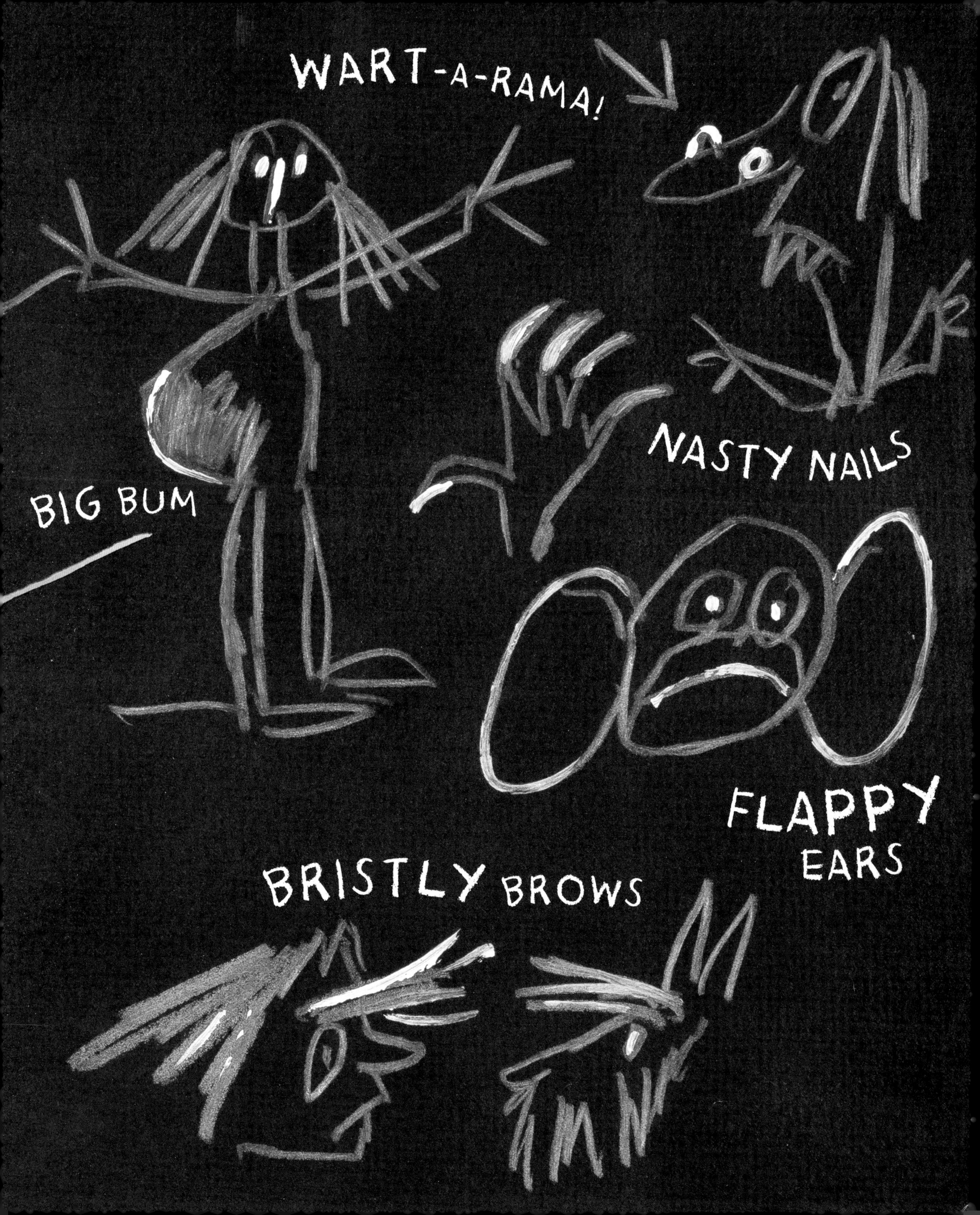
WART-A-RAMA!
NASTY NAILS
BIG BUM
FLAPPY EARS
BRISTLY BROWS

"Katy Carruthers! Good heavens, your brows are
as scruffy as any I've seen on a **Schnauzer**."

"Abigail Snape? You have ears like an ape!
Keep still while I stick them back neatly with tape."

"Nigel? Just look at your nails! They're in tatters.
Scrub them and file them. Yes, Nigel, it matters!"

"Miss Worthington? Kindly get rid of your **warts**.
And **Binky**? Your bottom's **too big** for those shorts."

No one was safe from Lucinda's advice.

"Grandpa!" she said. "Your **moustache** isn't nice.

Sit down and don't fidget, I'll give it a trim.

Grandma, you're next when I've finished with him."

Lucinda Belinda got hold of the cat.

"No kitten of mine goes out looking like that!

Look at your fur! It's all over the place.

Relax while I style it to flatter your face."

Whenever Lucinda
Belinda left home,
she carried her **mirror** and **tweezers** and **comb.**

Off she would go, with a smile on her face
to make the whole world a more beautiful place.

All very **charming** and *lovely* and *good*...
till she met with a MONSTER who lived in the wood.

A terrible, horrible, HIDEOUS BEAST.

Wasn't she terrified?

Not in the least!

"Goodness, you're ugly," she said. "You're a mess!
Your shoes and your handbag don't go with your dress.
Your fur is all filthy! Your fangs are a fright!"
(She showed it her teeth, which were pearly and white.)

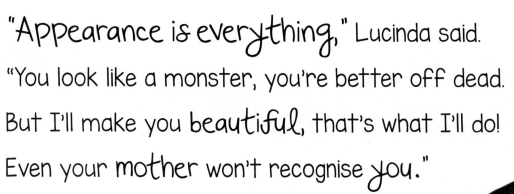

"Appearance is everything," Lucinda said.
"You look like a monster, you're better off dead.
But I'll make you beautiful, that's what I'll do!
Even your mother won't recognise you."

Before the poor monster
could give a reply,
she washed it and trimmed it
and blew its hair dry.

It was painted and preened,
it was powdered and primped.
It was shaved, it was sprayed,
it was styled, it was crimped.

"There!" she declared.
"Now you're truly divine."
Your face?
Why, it's almost as
pretty as mine.
"Now you are beautiful,
we can be friends."

But sadly, not all stories have happy ends...

"FRIENDS?" roared the monster.

"Lucinda, YOU'RE MAD!

under this 'beautiful me'

I'M STILL BAD!"

"My hair may be fair but my heart is still DARK.
And my minty-fresh FANGS
can still BITE like a SHARK.
My MONSTROUS mind is still BLACK as a cinder.
So now I must..."

And that's what it did.

Though it looked like a saint,

you can't change a monster

with powder and paint!